STARRING
Miss Darlene

WRITTEN, PRODUCED AND DIRECTED BY
AMY SCHWARTZ

A NEAL PORTER BOOK
ROARING BROOK PRESS
NEW MILFORD, CONNECTICUT

To Jane Feder

A Neal Porter Book

Published by Roaring Brook Press

Roaring Brook Press is a division of Holtzbrinck Publishing Holdings Limited Partnership

143 West Street, New Milford, Connecticut 06776

www.roaringbrookpress.com

Distributed in Canada by H. B. Fenn and Company, Ltd.

Library of Congress Cataloging-in-Publication Data

Schwartz, Amy.

Starring Miss Darlene/ Amy Schwartz.— 1st ed.

p. cm.

"A Neal Porter book."

Summary: Much to her surprise, a young girl's on-stage mishaps are reviewed favorably by the theater critic.

ISBN-13: 978-1-59643-230-7   ISBN-10: 1-59643-230-6

[1. Theater—Fiction. 2. Actors and actresses—Fiction. 3. Humorous stories.]   I. Title.

PZ7.S406St 2007   [E]—dc22   2006032177

Roaring Brook Press books are available for special promotions and premiums.

For details, contact: Director of Special Markets, Holtzbrinck Publishers.

Printed in China

First edition August 2007

10 9 8 7 6 5 4 3 2 1

THEATER CLASS

Darlene wanted to be a star. So she signed up for theater class.
The first morning, the director held auditions.
Darlene played Little Red Riding Hood.

After lunch, the director spoke to the class. "We'll be performing *Noah's Ark*."

"Jonathan, you're Noah," he said. "And Mary Ann, you're Noah's wife. William and Bethany are the Elephants, Mortimer and Sarah, the Giraffes, and Luke and Penelope, the Snakes. Darlene, you're the Flood."

All afternoon the actors practiced their parts. Darlene waited. She didn't know what the Flood should do.

In the evening she tried to act stormy in front of her mirror.

The next day the director pulled Darlene aside.

"You will be offstage holding a pan of water," he said. "When it's time for the Flood, you *dash* onstage and *throw* the water on the ground. It's simple, yet vital.

"You don't need to rehearse. What could go wrong?"

All week the actors rehearsed. Darlene crocheted an afghan.

On Friday, Darlene got dressed in a long blue gown that was her costume. She took her place backstage next to her pan of water.

"Look," the director said. "The theater critic from *The Daily Weekly* is in the front row."

The play started. Noah heard about the flood.
He built his ark. He gathered the animals.
He said, "It looks like rain."

Darlene *dashed* onstage.

Her feet got tangled
in her gown.
She spun around.

She *threw* the water.

Unfortunately she threw it into the front row.

On Sunday, Darlene opened the newspaper. "AUDIENCE PARTICIPATION," the headline read. "AN EXTREME SPORT."

"For this reviewer," the article continued, "Friday's show was a drenching, yet refreshing experience. Miss Darlene's performance was especially exciting."

Darlene read on, under her afghan, where it was nice and dry.

OUTER SPACE

On Monday the director said, "This week we will perform a science fiction play."

Darlene was very interested. She loved outer space.

"Jonathan," the director said, "will play Commander Whittaker. Mary Ann will play Ensign O'Forrest. William and Bethany, Mortimer and Sarah, and Luke and Penelope, the space aliens."

"And Darlene will be Professor Looney." The director handed out the scripts.

Darlene had thirteen lines!

She started rehearsing right away with the space aliens.

Darlene rehearsed on her way home,

at dinner,

and in front of the TV.
"The aliens have landed!" she
said. "The world has ended!"

The next day the director said
to Darlene, "Do you think you'll
have a problem with remembering
your lines?"

"Oh no! Not at all!" she replied.

She rehearsed while she
brushed her teeth . . .

and while she got dressed.
"We will rebuild our cities!"
Darlene threw out her arms.
"Our rivers will flow again!"

She rehearsed through her lunches,

in the bathtub,

and when she walked the dog.
"We have to begin again!" she
said. "We mustn't give up hope!"

On Friday, Darlene kept rehearsing as she climbed into her costume and put on her makeup.

The play began. The aliens landed. The world ended. Commander Whittaker, Ensign O'Forrest and Professor Looney entered.

"Professor Looney! What's happened???" Commander
Whittaker said.

Professor Looney looked out into the audience. She saw
the theater critic. Professor Looney froze.

"Professor Looney! What's happened???" Commander Whittaker said again.

"Uh-h-h-h," Professor Looney said.

"Professor Looney, what's happened to the human race???" Commander Whittaker repeated.

"The world has landed!" Professor Looney said. "The aliens
are ended! We have to give up hope! We mustn't begin again!"
Professor Looney crossed the stage. She threw out her arms.
"We will rebuild our rivers! Our cities will flow again!"

On Sunday, Darlene opened the newspaper. "PROFOUND PROFESSOR LOONEY," the headline read, "DEEPENS PLAY'S MYSTERY."

"In her role as Professor Looney," the article continued, "Miss Darlene used words in a way this reviewer has never even dreamed of. A triumph."

A mysterious smile crossed Darlene's face.

SLEEPING BEAUTY

"This week," the director said, "I will let one of you take over my job."

Jonathan and Mary Ann sat forward.

"Darlene, you're in charge," the director said.

Darlene couldn't believe her good fortune.

"We will perform *Sleeping Beauty*," she said.
"*I* will be Sleeping Beauty.

"Mary Ann, Penelope and Bethany are the fairy godmothers."

Darlene batted her eyelashes at Jonathan.

"And Jonathan is the Prince."

Darlene had never enjoyed rehearsals this much. Every day she pretended to be a sleeping princess. Every day Jonathan woke her up with a kiss.

The night before the performance Darlene couldn't sleep. Did the fairy godmothers know their lines? Would her costume fit? What would the theater critic think?

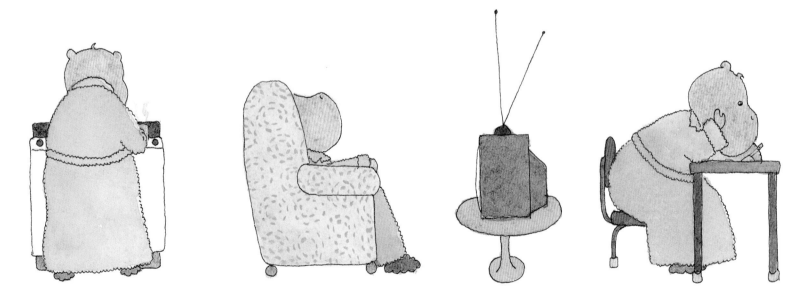

At midnight she made herself a mug of warm milk.
She watched some TV. She did a crossword puzzle.

Darlene played with her dog.

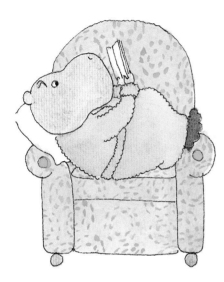

She read a book.

She stared into space.

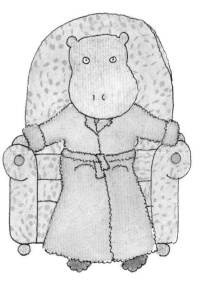

At last she fell asleep.

Darlene ran to theater class in the morning.
She had overslept.

She hurried into her costume,
trying not to yawn.

Darlene parted the curtains.
The theater critic was in his
usual spot.

The play began. Sleeping Beauty was born.
The fairy godmothers made their predictions. Sleeping Beauty grew up.

Darlene lay down on
Sleeping Beauty's bed.
It was very comfortable.

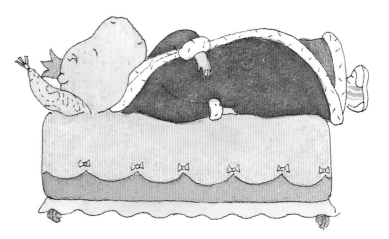

Sleeping Beauty fell asleep.
The Prince rode in.
"I will now wake Sleeping
Beauty," he said.
He kissed Sleeping Beauty.
Sleeping Beauty turned over.

"I will *now* wake Sleeping
Beauty!" the prince said.
He kissed Sleeping
Beauty again.
Sleeping Beauty snored.

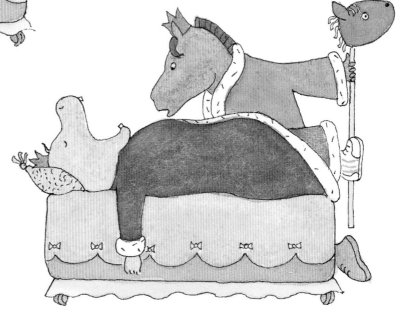

The Prince gave Sleeping
Beauty a kick.

Sleeping Beauty snorted
and woke up.

"What the . . ." said Sleeping
Beauty.

"The End," said the Prince.

On Sunday, Darlene opened the newspaper. "SLUMBERING PRINCESS," the headline read. "ENLIVENS CLASSIC PLAY."

"What could have been a tired production," the review continued, "instead had a whole new twist. Sleeping Beauty actually slept."

Darlene sat up on the sofa.

"With Miss Darlene," she read aloud, "A STAR IS BORN."